I Can Be Anything!

DON'T TELL ME I CAN'T

Diane Dillon

THE BLUE SKY PRESS

An Imprint of Scholastic Inc.

THE BLUE SKY PRESS

Celebrating 25 Years of Award-winning Publishing

Library of Congress catalog card number: 2017003956

ISBN 978-1-338-16690-3

10 9 8 7 6 5 4 3 2 1   18 19 20 21 22

Printed in China 38
First edition, March 2018

Book design by Kathleen Westray

For Bonnie,

the encouraging and loving voice

⌣

And to Maeve and Harper,

who are just beginning the journey

to know all they can be

THIS BOOK IS DEDICATED

TO DISCOURAGING

THE FRIGHTENED,

NEGATIVE LITTLE VOICE

IN OUR HEADS

THAT KEEPS US FROM

BEING ALL WE CAN BE.

"I can be anything I want to be."
Zoe stretched her arms and
spun around.

"I'm a bird. I can fly way up high,
floating on the wind!"

What if you fall? said a little voice.

"I won't fall. Birds have
wings. If my wings
get tired, I can fly in a
rocket ship to a faraway planet.

I'll meet planet people and have a tea
party before I come home."

What if you can't get home? said the voice.

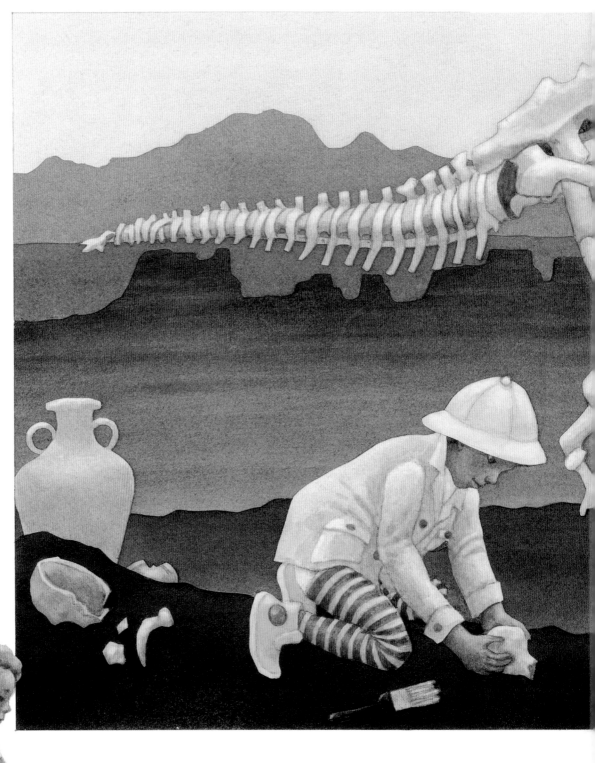

Zoe ignored the voice. "I can be an archeologist and travel around the world, and dig up dinosaur bones and buried treasures."

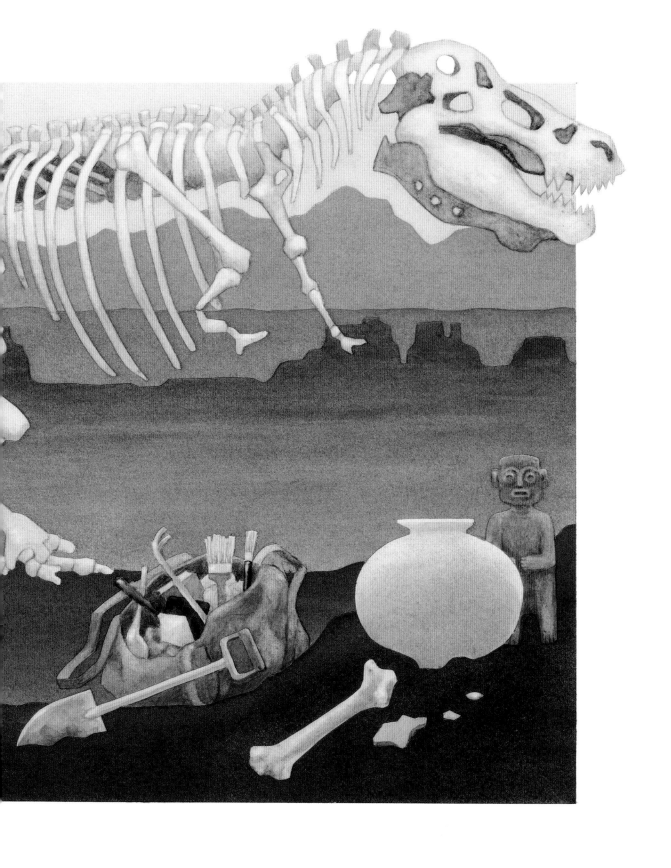

What if you get homesick?
You're too little, said the voice.

"No, I'm not. I'm bigger than you. Maybe I'll be a scientist and discover things, or I'll be an inventor and build a robot that will talk louder than you — so I won't hear you."

The voice was quiet for a while.

"I'll be a veterinarian and help wild animals like tigers and bears and dragons, and I'll give them medicine to make them well, and I'll bandage their hurts."

What if they bite you? said the voice.

"I'll be so gentle they won't bite me.
They will know I am helping them."

"Oh, I know. I'll be a fire girl and rescue people. I'll drive a big fire engine with a loud siren that goes *weoooo, weoooo,* and rescue a kitty stuck in a tree."

You can't drive a fire engine.
That's silly, said the voice.

"That's not silly. I can be anything I want to be, and don't tell me I can't. I'll be an artist and paint pictures, and a museum will hang them up so people can see them."

What if you don't have talent?
said the voice.

"Everybody has talent for something, and so do I. Besides, I'm smart. I can do anything if I try hard enough, and you won't stop me.

I can even be an ornithologist who
studies birds, or an oceanographer
who explores the ocean . . .

. . . or I can be a musician and give concerts all around the world.

I can even be President if I want to be.
You're just a voice, and I don't have
to listen to you."

*But I'm always with you, you know,
said the voice. No matter what you do.*

"You better be quiet, or I'll be an alligator and eat you up!" said Zoe.

The voice didn't have an answer to that. It was silent again.

"I can be an astronomer and study the stars

with a big telescope and discover new planets."

"I'll be a famous chef and bake fancy cakes as tall as I am, and I'll write a book about my recipes."

You can't write,
the voice came back.

"But I'm going to learn how to write in school.
Maybe I'll be a teacher and teach other kids
how to write, or I'll be a librarian and have
a zillion books to share with everyone."

You don't know what you want to be,
do you? said the voice.

"Go away, voice. I won't listen to you.
I'm not grown-up yet. I can be anything . . .

. . . but first I have to learn to read . . .
and read . . . and read! And I'll read books
about all the things I can be.
Don't tell me I can't!"